FOR JOE
—J.S.

FOR CURTIS AND BEN,
SASHA AND JESSAMIN,
NAT AND DEBORAH,
AND CATMANDU (the best fly-catcher in the business)
—E.K.

The Library of Congress has cataloged the hardcover edition of this work as follows:
Sierra, Judy.
Thelonius Monster's sky-high fly pie / by Judy Sierra; illustrations by Edward Koren.
p.   cm.
Summary: A good-natured monster thinks a pie made out of flies would be a good dessert and invites all his friends and relatives over to try it.
ISBN 978-0-375-83218-5 (trade) — ISBN 978-0-375-93218-2 (lib. bdg.)
[1. Monsters—Fiction. 2. Pies—Fiction. 3. Stories in rhyme.] I. Koren, Edward, ill. II. Title.
PZ8.3.S577Th2006
[E]—dc22
2005016773

ISBN 978-0-375-85949-6 (pbk.)

MANUFACTURED IN CHINA

10 9 8 7 6 5 4 3 2

First Dragonfly Books Edition

THELONIUS MONSTER'S SKY-HIGH FLY PIE

A revolting rhyme

by Judy Sierra

with delicious drawings

by Edward Koren

Dragonfly Books
New York

THELONIUS MONSTER

once swallowed a *fly,*

and decided that flies would taste

grand in a **pie.**

That silly guy!

THELONIUS urgently

e-mailed a spider.

He wanted advice from a savvy insider.

"You'll need something sticky" was her reply.

"To catch a fly."

THELONIUS MONSTER concocted a goo

of molasses and sugar and honey and glue,

and he rolled out a crust of astonishing size.

Now for the flies . . .

WANTED
FLIES
ONLY

THELONIUS stealthily followed

a

horse

and a

dog

and a
cat

and a
cow...

. . . and, of course, he dived in a Dumpster,

he circled a sewer,

and spent several hours near a pile of manure.

He lured **h u n d r e d s**

and **t h o u s a n d s**

of **succulent** flies,

and their footsies all stuck

to his fly-catching pie.

Perhaps they'll die.

PLEASE COME TO MY MANSION
THIS SUNDAY FOR PIE.

DON'T WEAR A TIE.

On Sunday, THELONIUS opened the door

to *eleventeen*

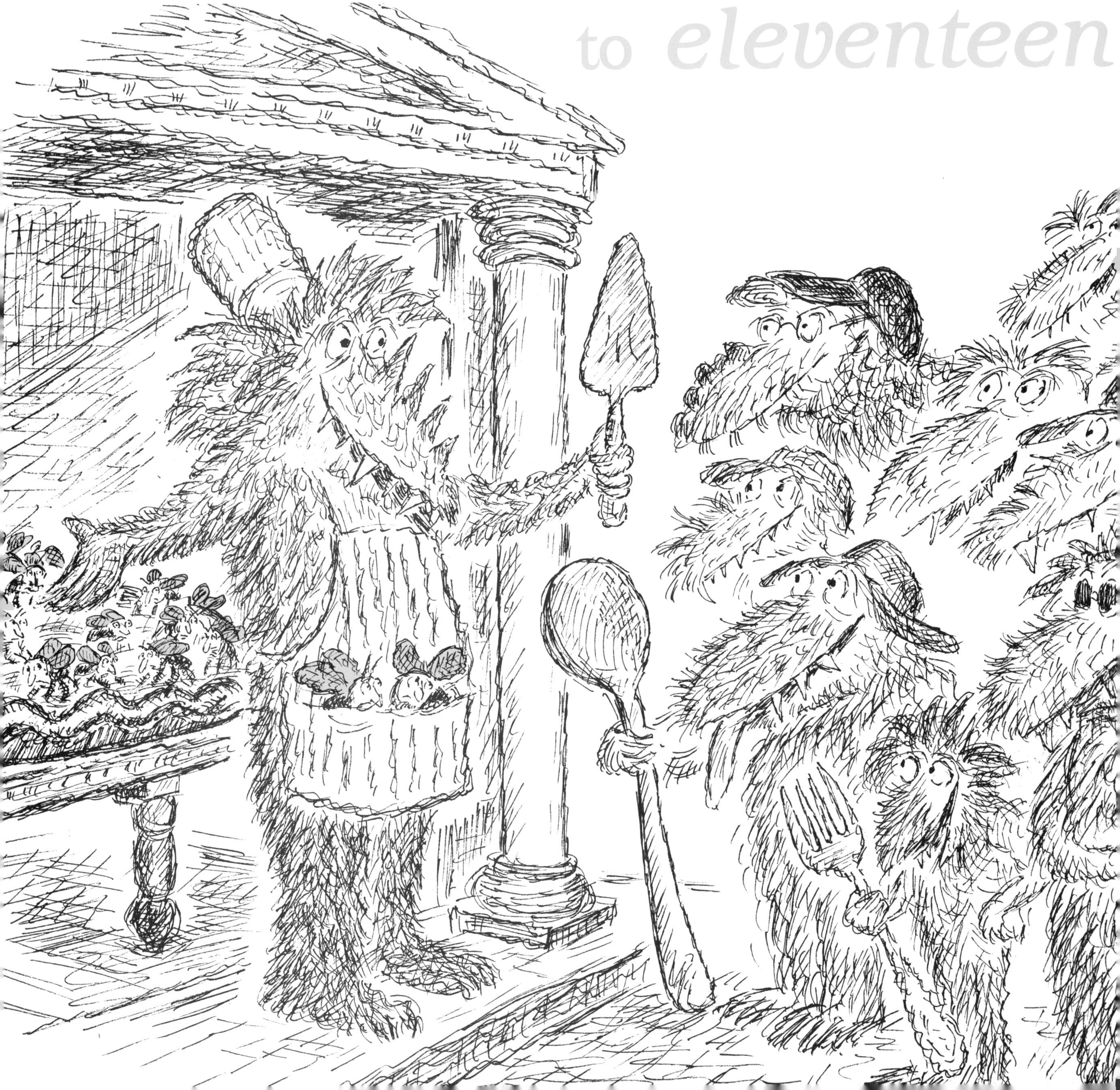

ravenous

m o n s t e r s ,

or more—

his aunties,

his uncles,

his cousins,

his chums.

"How it glistens!"

they shouted. "And listen—

it hums!

It's the tunefullest pie

that has ever been made.

We shall march to the

buzz in a

monster

parade."

As they picked up their forks

and they circled the room,

the pie full of flies lifted off with a

VOOM.

Up, up the staircase

it *whirred* and it *whined*

with all of the monsters galumphing behind.

It *whizzed* out the window.

It *whooshed* to the sky.

Bye-bye, fly pie!

THELONIUS MONSTER started to cry,

"Now no one will taste my

sensational pie."

(For though it had taken him so long to make it,

the monster had somehow forgotten to bake it.)

But then, by a stroke
of incredible luck,
in the sky all the flies'
little feet came unstuck.

When the pie *fell*
to earth in a
huge cloud
o f   d u s t ,
e l e v e n t e e n
monsters
devoured the crust.

His creepiest cousin declared with a roar,

"A DESSERT LIKE THIS

NEVER EXISTED BEFORE—

A PIE THAT COULD SPARKLE,

COULD SING, AND COULD SOAR.

IT'S DESPICABLY SWEET

(WITH A SLIGHT HINT OF FLY).

YOU'RE A FABULOUS COOK!

YOU'RE A WONDERFUL GUY!"

"We love your pie!"